FROM PORTABLE DAYS

FROM PORTABLE DAYS

A Personal Account of Life in the Theatre

by
Violet Godfrey Carr
as told to
Neil McNicholas

Foreword by Roy Hudd

THE SPREDDEN PRESS
STOCKSFIELD 1991

Published 1991 by
The Spredden Press
Brocksbushes Farm
Stocksfield
Northumberland NE46 7WB

Printed and bound by
SMITH SETTLE
Ilkley Road, Otley, West Yorkshire LS21 3JP

Contents

Foreword

My Lords, Ladies and Gentlemen! It gives me great pleasure to introduce Vi Godfrey's smashing little book. My own introduction to Vi's early days was through a talk she gave on Radio Newcastle a few years back. It was a tantalising glimpse into an almost forgotten world, a world even *I* don't remember! Now, with the help of Neil McNicholas, Vi has written it all down so that we will never forget.

Vi was born in the early years of the century and was 'at it', as we say in the profession, on stage from the age of three, actually playing parts! She began in the Portables, a form of theatre I knew nothing about, but her vivid memories and graphic descriptions of the 'theatre on wheels' soon bring those harsh, yet oh! so rewarding, days to vibrant life. Those were the days when performers had to take their show, and their theatre, to the public. Little market towns, village greens, anywhere they could drum up an audience. They were tough days indeed, as you will read, tough but totally fascinating.

Vi's career has been a unique one. It is a history of twentieth-century entertainment. 'Fits ups', black-faced entertaining, pierrots, singing booths, 'rep', working men's clubs, nightclubs, radio and television. Her pedigree is an immaculate theatrical one. One uncle was Teddy Knox, arguably the most talented of all The Crazy Gang, and another was Sax Rohmer, the creator of Fu Manchu. She married the King of Weston-super-Mare seaside entertainment, Will Godfrey. Will was a legend in those parts. His inventiveness, wit and talent for 'packing 'em in' was second to none. He'd even purposely misspell one word on a poster so people would look at it twice!

I know you'll enjoy this informative, moving and highly entertaining story. It is the story of the real, hard-working professional who loved the game and, as Vi herself says, 'always tried to look on the funny side of things – that is the meaning of trouper'. I agree, because Vi was, and is, the ultimate trouper.

Roy Hudd
Septmber 1991

Introduction

Violet Godfrey Carr began her theatrical career as a baby, lying in her mother's arms, on-stage in her family's own theatre. It almost ended during the Second World War when she lay across an unexploded bomb, in the wreckage of a cinema.

Ever the trouper, neither the trauma of that experience nor the serious injuries resulting from it could permanently dampen her spirits or her career. She had been born into the particularly tough world of the Portable Theatre which, as the name implies, consisted of mobile theatre groups. Come hail, rain or shine, they brought their entertainment to wherever the people were, and they also brought their theatre with them!

Because permanent theatres were restricted to London and the larger towns and cities, the Portable Theatre was one way for the more ambitious professionals of the day to bring drama and entertainment to villages and communities off the beaten track and in the rural areas. It would seem that very little is remembered about the Portables so that part of Violet's story may be all the more valuable to those interested in the history of the theatre.

As modes of transport improved in the early decades of this century, Portable Theatres gave way to Fit Up Companies. These provided virtually the same forms of entertainment but did so over a much wider area and used established facilities for the performances. Church and village halls were literally fitted up as theatres.

More and more people followed the Victorians and Edwardians to the seaside, and small companies of entertainers began to set up stage on the sands at resort towns. The first of these were the minstrel shows, leading on later to the Pierrots, and eventually to the more permanent forms of seaside variety shows still popular today.

Although the compiling and production of this text has been very much a cooperative venture between Violet and myself, I would like to acknowledge and thank her for that cooperation and for making available the various sources which were essential to it.

The core of the text is an account that she wrote for herself in 1982 which provided a very informative survey of her career on the stage and her personal reflections on her many and varied experiences in the

Violet Godfrey Carr, c.1938.

theatre. To this then were added other recollections and incidents transcribed from a series of taped interviews which she had done for local radio in the late 1970s, as well as the fruits of our conversations in working together on this project.

Vi also gave me access to such personal mementos as had survived the wartime bombings in which, very sadly, so many of her things were lost. These included a selection of photographs and playbills and her husband Will's press book.

Violet's story is an often light-hearted, at times very poignant, personal account of her career treading the boards. It also provides a very interesting historical picture of the theatre from the turn of the century – indeed, from Portable days.

Neil McNicholas

THE EARLY YEARS

Jenny Parker, daughter of a Northumberland squire, left home in 1892. Jenny was my mother. She was a trained vocalist and had a very beautiful voice. Much against her family's wishes she went to London to do concert work, and was most successful. Though she had no training in drama – formal training was unheard of at this time, and strolling players of the day had only talent and love of drama to urge them on – Jenny decided this was what she wanted most in life. It was in London that she met and married my father, George Austin Knox, who was from an old theatrical family in London, descended from the Scottish reformer John Knox.

Theatres were rare outside London although there were the old style music halls. The cinema as such did not exist. The class entertainment of the day in the provinces was the Portable Theatre. The 'Penny Gaff' was on the go at the same time as the Portable but shouldn't be confused with it. The Penny Gaff was basically just a slide show accompanied by a talk on the subject of the slides. When it was finished, a mock auction was held. The slide show brought the people in but the whole idea was to sell them things. The Portable Theatre was clearly much better value at sixpence, with seven or eight players putting on a good quality drama with songs and a farce.

My mother suggested doing theatre specifically for the miners up in Durham; she was, of course, aware of the need for entertainment in the mining communities. They therefore came up with the rather adventurous idea of putting together a Portable Theatre and taking it up to the North-East. So it was, then, that in the 1890s my mother and father started their Portable Theatre in Durham, and eventually elsewhere in the Northumberland area. Although Knox was the family name, they called theirs the Austin Theatre. Miners have always been a critical audience, they especially know good singing, so one had to provide entertainment to their taste in order to draw the crowds. This the Austins did with much success, and they brought together a small but talented band of players.

After my father died in 1908 (in Gateshead), Mother was left to cope

Jenny and George Austin Knox.

with the Portables, a family of five, and another baby – me – on the way. I was born at Tow Law, County Durham on 23 July 1908. From birth I was very sickly and at two weeks old was brought to Ushaw Moor when my mother's Portable moved from Tow Law. In poor health herself, she walked the streets of the village looking for somewhere to stay. A kindly person noticed her and how very tired she looked and asked her indoors. So it was that the Carrs came into my life – the couple who were to become my foster-mother and -father.

When the time came for the theatre to move on, I was still in poor health. With a family to look after and a Portable to control, Mother felt it would be too much and the doctor advised that I be left behind. The Carrs volunteered to care for me – and a more genuine and generous couple one could never find anywhere. With only one daughter of their own – Lizzie, then sixteen – I was truly fussed over.

Those early years were very confusing for me. Because I grew up living with the Carrs I thought they were my real parents and didn't realize that it was actually my Mother who kept sending for me whenever she needed

Mam and Dad Carr with their daughter Lizzie (Flatley).

a child actor. I was carried on stage for the first time at a fortnight old — they wanted a baby and I was it. By the time I was three, I was already playing actual parts. Quite a start for an old trouper! It would be seven years before Mother returned to Ushaw Moor to take a lease on a cinema in the village. It was only then that I found out that she was my real mother.

Work really started for me when she began her season of plays. There were so many plays with children's parts in them in those days: child interest was very important. I went to local schools and studied child parts in between, and Mother, being the splendid actress she was, did not spare my tuition. In every part I had to be 'DLP' – dead-letter-perfect. She was very strict and every move on stage had to be perfect too. Later in life I was very grateful for this training.

Violet and friends (Violet is standing, wearing a bow).

'Portable people' always had their families with them and so there were always children in the group. Life wasn't easy for them. They had to share the chores – everyone mucked in – and perhaps play children's parts as well. For example, in addition to the parts I played, one of my regular chores was combing out the feathers on the shire horses' hooves; those wonderful horses were our constant companions.

What I remember most as a child was not having much playtime because apart from having to go to school – that was the law – you also had to study your part for the evening performance, and you had to be good at it. Also, from the age of three, I was taught by my mother how to put on my own make-up! That may sound incredible, but in those days that's how it was.

School ended at three o'clock, then there would be a rehearsal and you had your part to learn for the next play! In a way this was a form of further education. To begin with you learned all the big words in the script, words you hadn't yet learned at school. You really can't act a part unless you know what you are talking about, so everything was explained. In addition you also learned singing and dancing.

The performances were scheduled according to the times of the shifts at the pit – you had to do that. The night shift men would never see a play ordinarily so, if you put on a little show for them in the morning, Mother would have to go to the school and explain. Taking children out of school was always avoided wherever possible so as to keep right with the authorities. Inspectors would often visit the Portable to see what the conditions were like, and how the children were being cared for. Parents were parents in those days, and they kept their children with them wherever they went. They were good family people.

Of course we children went from school to school as the show moved around. School days were not too comfortable because, being theatrical, we were looked upon as somehow different and as such were ostracised. Nowadays stage and television personalities are looked upon as little gods, as something special, but in the era I am talking about 'theatricals' were thought of as roaming gypsies and not nice to know. I felt this very much at school – children can be cruel with each other – and in fact I have no happy memories of school days. Very often catty remarks were made about my mother being on the stage, and about my putting 'paint' on my face. Nice people didn't use make-up.

Teachers also saw me as being someone apart, yet when there was a charity concert to be given by the school children I was always expected to be involved because of my experience of singing and dancing, and stagecraft in general. At some time each day, instead of lessons, I was sent to teacher's room to instruct the other children in those things, and during the production I was rarely off stage and worked very hard.

At an early age, I was also busy performing for charity and in competitions. During the period of the First World War, I took part in concerts for wounded soldiers – so called At Homes – and as a child performer was very popular all over the county. I was kept busy singing such songs of the time as 'Sergeant Daddy V.C.' and 'Keep the Home Fires Burning', and dancing the hornpipe, sword dance and skipping rope dances on an illuminated glass pedestal. There were no dancing schools as they are today. One learned by trial and error.

I remember that 'go-as-you-please' talent competitions were in vogue all over the county, and I used to enter them. It was the time of silent

Violet, aged 10.

films, and the talent spot would come between the first film and the main feature. More often than not I was the only child competitor and, with my experience and talent, I always won. I well remember male competitors rowing with the management about the unfair competition – 'A kid always gets the sympathy of the audience'! I would stand in the middle of it all bewildered: that sort of thing made me dread competitions. Nevertheless I appeared.

I was nine when my mother moved on once again. She decided that, because I was the youngest of the family, I was still useful for child parts and so this time I should go with her. Needless to say I was by then very much attached to my foster parents but, much as they didn't want to lose me, they had no claim over me and could do nothing about it. On a Sunday morning, with the theatre packed on the cart, we moved off to

6

Broughs, the grocers, c.1925 (Violet is 5th from the right).

Murton Colliery and settled in digs. I knew the play my mother was going to do and I knew that she needed me for it, but I was sick of it all. Within two weeks I realised how very much I was missing Mam and Dad Carr and Ushaw Moor and, remembering Mother's strict and austere attitude, I decided not to stay! I left Murton and, because there were no buses, set out to walk the fourteen miles to Ushaw Moor. This may sound incredible but it is nevertheless true. I managed to get as far as Durham when, exhausted, I was spotted by some miners from Ushaw Moor who recognised me as 'Jenny Austin's girl', and they carried me the rest of the way.

That ended contact with Mother for some years. I also lost touch with my brothers and sisters and years passed without news of Mother or family.

I continued to be involved in entertainment locally. Then, in 1922, at the age of fourteen, I left school and immediately had to start earning as Mam and Dad Carr were by this time pensioners and ten shillings (50p) a week was all they got. For a while I worked as a lather girl at the local barber's for a few shillings, then for about four years at 'Broughs', a local grocer, a job which at that time was considered quite an opportunity at thirteen shillings (65p) a week!

I gave eleven shillings to the Carrs and, on the remaining two shillings, bought my own clothes and later paid for singing lessons from Mr J. Lisle of the Durham Cathedral Choir. Mr Lisle was in the audience at a church charity show one day when I was singing in front of the curtain while scenery was being changed. He came backstage to ask whether I might be interested in taking voice training lessons. He gave me his card. I was duly tried for voice range and began weekly lessons. As I progressed my teacher was very pleased with my voice and I became lady soloist with the Cathedral Quartet which gave me my first taste of opera. Doing 'good class' – what would now be called first class – concert work was excellent experience.

By 1924 silent films had brought about an increase in cinemas and, at about the age of sixteen, I was fortunate in getting an engagement singing to the films. This involved singing background songs appropriate to particular scenes, and I did this work throughout the region wherever the particular films were being shown. Typical of those films were *The White Sister*, *Smiling Thro'*, *The Rosary*, and *Parted*, to mention just a few. The fee I received helped me further my training.

As the years that would be known as the Depression approached, the outlook in the mining areas became increasingly bleak with strikes and hard times. I was busy in concerts raising money for the Boot Fund which provided the children of miners with shoes, and also for the soup kitchens where children could have at least one cooked meal a day. It was also a very worrying time for me, without any prospects. My wage at the grocer's was not enough, and Mam and Dad had enough of a struggle without my adding to it. Besides, their only daughter and her husband and family were also living with them so room was scarce. I knew it was time for me to move, but where would I go?

It was at about this time (November 1927) that news arrived of my mother's death. By then my two brothers William and George Knox, and two sisters Rose (Goulding) and Frances (whom I never knew as she had been adopted by the Glaxo family), were married but were no longer involved in theatre. There had always been a degree of rivalry between us kids for parts, but I think I had more 'theatre' in me. They played their parts, but not with the same enthusiasm that I had. I always put my heart into my work and I think that's why I carried on in what can often be a very hard profession.

Bob (Austin Knox) Cromwell – Violet's uncle. His variety/
revue double act, with his daughter Mini, was well-known in
the Northeast.

2

THE PORTABLE THEATRE

Portable Theatres were always individually made. My father would have gone to a woodworker and told him exactly how he wanted it to be. They would be designed to the same basic principles, being as near as possible like a real theatre, but each one would have its own particular character and construction.

The Austins' were comfortable, with red plush and gilt much in evidence to create atmosphere. The top (the roof) was of canvas held by guy ropes, and the side walls were panels of highly polished mahogany. They fitted one in the other as slats, and screwed down into a strong wooden floor into which red tip-up seats were also fastened down. These were the best seats, the cheaper rear seats were usually just wooden benches. The proscenium consisted of heavy red-plush curtains draped artistically with tassels and baubles which looked most effective. The stage was about the size of a small village hall stage – quite big enough – and the wings screwed down into it. The stage lighting consisted of naphthalene footlights, an enormous improvement on the oil lamp and 'limelight' spots that tended to spit carbon all over the stage. We dressed at the side of the stage as there were no dressing-rooms.

Travelling between village sites was slow and often very cold on open carts drawn by shire horses. The carts were piled high with scenery, hampers, and everything else, and the children of the players would be on top covered with a tarpaulin!

Because we travelled all through the winter, we had to be tough. We would try to find a place where we could stay for as long as possible – depending on how good business was – in order to avoid travelling in the bad weather. I remember, for instance, staying for quite a long time once on the green at West Auckland. Staying in one place also meant having to do several productions so it was a hard time in terms of the repertoire, playing one role while rehearsing for another. By and large it was all in the repetition – if you'd once done a part, it was all there to be recalled, but every day you had rehearsals just the same as in a proper theatre.

The Austin Theatre played at Ushaw Moor, Esh Winning, Cornsay,

Artist's impression of the interior of the Austin Theatre.

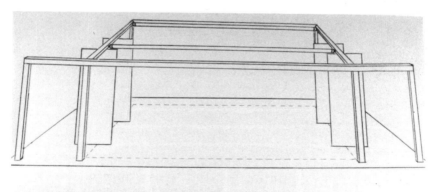

Stage framework assembled.

Quebec . . . all the places round and about which were then thriving mining communities. I don't remember ever going anywhere near the coast because the family had another Portable that covered that area.

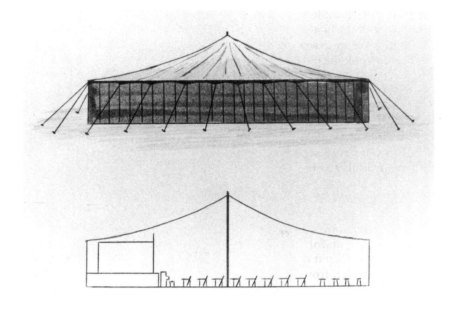

Marquee and interior.

Other Portable Theatres toured in other parts of the country – for example there was Goddard's in Wales, and a man called Jones in Scotland – but to my knowledge we were the only ones in the North-East. In fact we were the first ones to be heard of in this area, and the others were not as large as ours. The Austin Theatre was really done on a grand scale.

The arrival of a Portable was announced by an Advance Man whose job, apart from being one of the troupe, was to scout the best and most centrally located villages where good business would be likely. He then spread publicity for the coming visit. This consisted of handbills stuck on trees, as the circus did, and of going into the village pub and buying a round thus making himself (and the theatre) generally known – and popular!

Portables usually set up close to pubs because they tended to be at the centre of community life. They, in turn, were always good to us because of all the extra business we brought them. The village pub would generally also have spare rooms. (Mother and Father would never stay in a van – a caravan. I never remember a van of any description.) However, digs (lodgings) could be difficult to find because in those days people were wary of the 'actor fellow' – it was a case of 'bring in your daughter, the actors are in town' – but once the group were known to villagers, they really took the players to their hearts.

On arrival, the theatre was erected and everything left in order for the opening performance. Depending on the weather, that process could take four or five hours. We were obviously quite expert at it, but it was very hard work. This had to be done before giving a thought to where anyone would sleep that night. During the period of the Great War, theatre workers were very scarce so my mother painted her own scenery and donned overalls to erect and change scenes as required. She was quite a woman! Because all the men in the cast were too old for enlistment, they were also unsuitable for the part of the hero or the usually young leading man. But Mother did not let this deter her – 'the show must go on' – and, being tall and slim, she decided to play her own leading man, cutting quite a figure in uniform or evening dress.

Sometimes when it came to props you could borrow larger items, such as armchairs etc., from the pub, and you kept your eyes open for other likely props. People were very good about lending things. When you think of plays today and what we did then, we did marvellously.

We also had to make our own costumes, and I was taught at a very early age how to improvise by unstitching one costume and making it into something else. Although it was possible to make things look authentic from where the audience was sitting, Mother had a good stock of period and specialist costumes. Sundays were usually spent washing all the props and costumes in a tin bath in the auditorium, using hot water from the pub. Of course you avoided washing anything that would be needed on Monday and might not be dry in time, or you washed things only when there was a change in production. Everything was packed in wicker hampers which were not as heavy as trunks would have been when travelling. You carried your own personal belongings in your own bags, whatever type you had (Gladstones etc.). We all dressed as well off stage as on, something I still think is very important in the theatre. Off stage you were a walking advertisement for the company. You always behaved well, and you always looked as if you had a million dollars even if you hadn't got so much as the price of a cup of tea!

We never had the modern type of make-up, it was all real greasepaint in all the different colours. If you wanted black for eyelashes, for instance, you lit a piece of candle and, using an orange stick or a hairpin with black greasepaint moulded on, you put it through the candle and then onto your eyelashes. From time to time Mother would have to send someone to the nearest big city, which was about the only place where you'd be able to get proper make-up. Also you didn't have any of the fancy creams they have today for taking your make-up off, you used lard! You went out and bought it by the packet, scalded it in boiling water, and left it until the next day. After draining it you added lavender water to take away the smell!

Music was provided on the piano, but often there would be someone in the show who also played violin, banjo, or some other instrument because every *artiste*, as well as acting, had to be able to do 'a turn'. The drama was first and then the turns, with a farce to finish the show. The turns were singers: they did ballads, opera, etc., depending on the audience, and the children did song and dance. Invariably, also, there was someone who could play an instrument. The farce was the old-fashioned short comedy sketch.

Not only had the actors to be talented, they were troupers in the true sense of the word. They had to erect the theatre (no easy task in all weathers), change scenery at the end of each act, do the sound effects ('noises off'), and many times had to double up parts – being killed off early in the play only to return later as another character! They also looked after the horses which were the means of transport for the theatre.

Often in bad weather, especially if there was a gale, the play would be halted whilst players and audience would ease the guy ropes to stop the canvas top being damaged by the wind. Even so, occasionally the wind would be too strong and would take the entire roof off. The audience would then help out by chasing after it, bringing it back, and helping to secure it again. All this was taken as 'one of those things' and, when all was settled, the play would continue. My uncle, Teddy Knox, used to tell the Royal Family the story about being in the middle of the melodrama *Driven From Home* when all at once the wind carried off the canvas top and, as he said, 'We were all driven from home'! (Teddy Knox was a member of the Crazy Gang who were friends of the Royal Family, and for years entertained privately at Sandringham and Windsor.)

I really don't remember anything ever being a flop. I think people were so delighted to see this new form of entertainment come into their village that they accepted whatever was put on. Audiences would often get quite carried away by the play, booing and cheering, and sometimes even jumping up on the stage.

I always remember *The Sign of the Cross* at Easter, with my mother playing Mercia – they always said she was the finest Mercia in the

Teddy Knox – Violet's uncle.

business. We were always a little wary of the religious theme but the people seemed to love it. I played a little boy who at one point was on the rack and you would hear all kinds of sympathetic comments from the audience like, 'Ah . . . the poor little sod'! There was one occasion during a performance of *Jane Shaw* when the action called for the leading lady to be dragged along the street whilst being whipped. One of the miners jumped on the stage and shouted, 'Thou dee that again, yer bugger, and I'll kill yer!' and he snatched away the whip! Such was the spirit created by the shows.

It could be rather difficult trying to play over all these comments and disturbances. That was one of the first things that you learned on stage – that you never took any notice of what your audience was doing. Whether they were clapping you, or booing you, you had to carry on. You also got used to it: it was part of the plays, and the people loved them.

I don't think that company members ever really got involved in writing plays. All of ours were taken from Dick's *Penny Books*: *The Dumb Man of Manchester*; *Gypsy Queen*; *East Lynne*; *Maria Martin – Murder in the Red Barn*; *Sweeney Todd the Demon Barber*; *Uncle Tom's Cabin*; *The Face at the Window*; and *The Sign of the Cross*. We never did any Shakespeare, there was no call for it. Mother knew Shakespeare's plays but she would never have dreamed of putting them on. Education was poor in those days and you had to give the people something that they would understand. A different play would be performed each night and there were 'potted pantos' for the children's matinee at the weekend. If we happened to be in one place for a while and had exhausted our little rep of pantomimes, well then perhaps we'd get together and write something ready for the Saturday.

If you wanted extras for crowd work or for a special part, you could always find someone willing to do it. Nor was it any trouble finding miners who wanted to sing. If any of them asked to do a turn, Mother was very wise and would never turn them down. She'd ask them to come along the next night knowing that if she put them on stage there'd be a good house! Sometimes we would have extras who then wanted to come with us. I remember one chap from Ushaw Moor who decided he was going to do that, and when we got to the next place there he was. He wanted to act, and he could act: he was a natural. Of course you couldn't afford to pay extras, but that didn't matter to him. He stuck with us and I believe that later he did get into rep.

Occasionally, if you put on a classic, the gentry would come to see it. They would come behind the stage afterwards to see what kind of people we were who had come to their village. I remember that as a child I would stand in awe, looking them up and down, thinking how wonderful they were, especially the ladies in their furs!

Each evening, after the show, it was a recognised thing for performers to sally forth to the village pub where admirers from that night's audience would buy them drinks. At the same time it was important to mix with the people of the village, and my mother was good at that. After my father died, she took over and ran the Portables on her own – a tremendous thing for her to be doing. Although women didn't go in public bars in those days, and though my mother was a teetotaller, as the proprietor of the theatre she would go in the pub to meet the miners and buy them a round. The next day, at the mine, it would be spread around that we show people were all right, and that would encourage the miners to come to the show. It was common practice for the proprietor to have a credit list so that poeple could come to the show 'on tick'. Miners were paid fortnightly and often by the second week were broke. In almost every case those on tick paid up at the weekend.

It was the First World War that brought about the end of the Portables, primarily because there was no longer any call for them. In their place the Fit Up Theatres developed, but, sadly, it was the end of an era. For one thing there wasn't the same family feeling that there had been with the Portables – you weren't as close to the people. Then, we no longer stayed only in the North-East, in fact I never came back to County Durham in Fit Up. I was sorry to see the end of the portable Theatres because that was all I had ever known up to that time. I still get a very positive reaction from the older people of Ushaw Moor who remember the Portable being down by the Station Hotel. In its day there was nothing like it, nor is there anything like it today.

I remember I was playing a concert party in Skegness in about 1936, and happened to be talking about the end of the Portables. Someone asked whether I realised that there was still a Portable in operation in Lincolnshire. Needless to say I asked them to find out where it was playing and I went over in the car the next morning. Lo and behold, there it was, a Portable Theatre, right out in the middle of the sugar beet area. That was the last one I ever saw.

3
REP AND FIT UP COMPANIES

In about 1922, the son of one of the players from the Austin Theatre days was playing in Newcastle and came to Ushaw Moor to find out what had happened to me. With him was his friend Will Godfrey who, much later, was to become my husband. I was delighted to meet one of the old Portable associates, and he invited me to play a part during the rep season in Northumberland. This I did successfully and it encouraged me to think about going back into the profession, more especially in the light of my circumstances at that time.

Will Godfrey made a very handsome leading man, and from the start was keen to date me. The Sunday I was to return to Ushaw Moor after the show finished, Will came to my digs to say 'goodbye' and brought a lovely bunch of flowers. As I was admiring them, the lady next door came in and said, 'So you're the one who stole my flowers!' Was Will's face red! However all went off with a laugh. He saw me home to Durham, missed the last bus to Newcastle, and walked all the way back – adopting a stray dog along the way, he told me later. Letters came daily from wherever he was playing.

I continued to entertain locally, hoping to improve my situation, and at last Fate seemed to play her part when Gertrude Vickers' stock (or rep) company arrived at the village of Esh Winning just three miles away. One member of the company, a friend of my mother, came to visit my foster parents. I was so keen to see the performances that I walked the six miles! Just when they were ready to leave I was told that there was a vacancy for an 'actress/singer'. I did the audition and got the job – to play whatever part was required and all the singing needed, and to provide my own wardrobe – for two pounds a week. My wardrobe posed quite a problem as I had very little more than a change of street clothes and one semi-evening dress. Also I had no band parts for my songs and no money. However, I was not deterred and I packed my few belongings and travelled with the company overnight to Manchester.

Fortunately, for my first time away from home (it was 1927, I was just nineteen) I got very comfortable digs, a bed-sitter, buying my own food

Will Godfrey, c.1922.

which the landlady cooked – that was the thing pros often did. Although it was a good season, it was also financially very difficult trying to get together a wardrobe which had to be quite extensive in rep. We did twice-nightly performances, with a matinee, changing between two different plays during the week which meant studying and rehearsing for the next play whilst working in the current one. It was hard work but I enjoyed it, because for me it was simply a matter of doing what I had always done.

Then, one Saturday morning, there was a shock. Gertrude had collapsed and, due to her ill-health, the season was to end. As I had not saved any money this proved to be a considerable worry. I had to buy *The Stage* – the theatrical paper in which vacancies in show business are advertised – and there was also the expense of photographs to send when applying for work, to say nothing of the cost of stamps and professional paper. All this was a drain on my two weeks notice of closure, and, without a job, what could I do? I certainly couldn't return to Ushaw Moor with nothing because I would have been a financial burden on my foster parents. There was nothing to do but stay put: I signed on the dole and received fifteen shillings (75p) a week. I immediately put my cards on the table with the landlady and it was agreed that I should move to the attic and do household chores to pay for the rent and to keep myself in food whilst looking for work.

One morning, when I joined the dole queue, the clerk called me in to see the manager. My first thought was that my dole was to be stopped and, if that happened, what would I do? There was no Social Security at that time. However, to my delight, I was offered a temporary position as a dole clerk. I passed the necessary tests and started the following Monday. I made many friends in the office and was quite happy there, but I longed to get back to the theatre. I continued buying *The Stage* and writing for work. In the meantime, I scoured the markets for remnants and in the evenings made props, ever hopeful of getting back on stage. Besides, I knew my present job was only temporary and I wanted to be prepared.

My job did eventually come to an end but fortunately it wasn't long before I managed to find work with a Fit Up Company – a group of actors playing village halls, doing different plays each night, with variety and farce to follow the play and a matinee on Saturdays. It was a very similar routine to that of the old Portable days, even to each *artiste* helping to erect the 'fit up' frame on the stage and sometimes even the stage itself. As with the Portables, there was a pianist capable of playing background music (especially for sad scenes) before dashing round to make an entrance on stage. Also, whilst the actors were changing scenery, the pianist would keep the audience entertained. The Fit Up Theatre was very difficult work as you did a different play every night. If you could play Fit Ups, you could play anything.

Even by the time of the Fit Ups it could be difficult to find digs in a new area. People were still wary of theatrical folk until they got to know you. Many times we would have to make the best of a difficult situation, sleeping in the village hall where we were appearing, using the stage curtains as a bed, and 'enjoying' a makeshift meal. We were never miserable and tried to look at the funny side of things even when there wasn't one! That is the true meaning of trouper.

We didn't have a salary as such, it was shares – meaning one *artiste* one share. The manager got two shares, the extra one going towards scripts, scenery etc. The takings were equally divided after all expenses had been paid, which meant that each person had to do his or her best to draw the people in. This was done not only on stage but by mixing off stage too and by becoming popular. It could be to one's advantage to be liked off stage. Because most of the areas where we played were off the beaten track, and because we always had to provide our own food, the gift of a chicken or fresh eggs was very welcome.

The old Portable Theatres used to restrict themselves to certain regions because of the amount of equipment that had to be transported and because travel was by horse and cart. The Fit Up Theatres had better transportation and so they travelled further afield, and with audiences also being more mobile the Fit Ups could expect to draw from wider areas. They each had their own 'happy hunting grounds' which they visited — areas which were particularly good for business. For instance, Lincolnshire was a good area when sugar beet and potatoes were being picked because the locals made extra cash and really liked the melodramas.

After doing rep, it might seem that Fit Ups were a step down but that wasn't the case. Fit Ups were very popular after the First World War

Violet — Theatre Royal, Leicester
c.1930.

because they toured the smaller communities away from the cities and people were very appreciative of the entertainment they provided. I am certain that Fit Ups – like the Portable Theatre before them – were the finest training in stage craft that you could have. Even today there are stars on television and in the theatre who started in the Fit Ups. It is a pity that there is no such experience for beginners these days.

One of the companies I toured with at this time was Fred Webb's. I remember spending Christmas (1927 or '28) at Whitby rehearsing the lead in *My Sweetheart*, but right at the last moment Fred decided to bring his daughter to play the part instead. At least I had to be paid just the same but winter was hardly the time to be 'on holiday' in Whitby! Back in the lead after Whitby, I continued with Webb's but it was only a short tour.

By the summer of 1929 I was back in rep again and spent my twenty-first birthday playing a hall in Horden Colliery. From there I travelled to Leicester, where we had a particularly good run, and then on to Fleetwood. I still have two clippings from a Lancashire paper of the time which, although they mention my performances, are more interesting for the other names they bring back to mind:

'The Indian Prince' a musical comedy produced this week at the Fleetwood Palace Theatre, is a huge success. . . . The performers are excellent – good vocalists, funny comedians and graceful dancers.
    Mr. T. Gilbert Perry plays the mock Prince . . . and he is ably assisted by Miss Jessie Jones, a bright and sprightly Eliza. Charlie Parker is a comedian who pleases all. The vocal numbers are splendidly rendered by Miss Violet Carr and Mr. Fred Barnes, who gain encores nightly. . . .

(*The Indian Prince* was such a success that Perry asked the company to follow it with a season of rep. I asked for an advance on my salary, and I was able to bring Mam Carr over to Fleetwood for a holiday during part of the season as a little 'thank you'.)

Mr. T. Gilbert Perry, the manager of the Fleetwood Palace has given us a change of fare this week from musical to farcical comedy. The popular company engaged have proved themselves as excellent as ever in the screaming comedy 'The New Boy', a play that had such a successful run in London.
    It is impossible to single out artists for special praise, as all deserve it, but Miss Violet Carr has shown her versatility by being not only a sweet singer, but a

comedienne who charms everyone.

Next week will be presented the popular comedy drama 'A Lassie from Lancashire', and a special attraction on Friday night will be the ever-popular pathetic drama, 'East Lynne'.

It was after this run in Fleetwood that I ended up back in Fit Ups and, though I don't remember exactly why, it was a tour of southern Ireland with Kitty O'Shea's company. This was very different from England. Time seemed to be of little importance: we would often be made up ready to start at seven-thirty but were lucky if we got started by eight-thirty! However, when we did start it was always to a full house. My singing over there was very well received and unfortunately that led to problems. To begin with, I had been hired into an Irish family group and being the only English person in the party was not always pleasant, given the political problems between the two countries. But then we would sing curtain raisers before the drama and my singing began to receive more applause – and encores – than anyone else's, and this led to a great deal of jealousy. One day when I went to rehearsal I found that the company had gone and had left me stranded. I was politely told to get out of my digs, and for the first time I was left desolate in a strange country. It was, I believe, December 1929 and, managing to get back home, I spent Christmas in Ushaw Moor suffering from shingles!

Fit Up tours provided some interesting experiences.

Whilst we were playing at Immingham in Lincolnshire, a vicar came over to ask us to perform in his very small church hall at Limber and we agreed to do so. However, we found on arrival that there was only one exit and the fire officer said we couldn't play with the door closed in case there was a fire: a clear getaway was necessary. The village lads said, 'Right we'll take the door off', and this was duly done and a heavy curtain hung to stop the draught. At another church hall, with everything ready to begin, the only 'person' in the audience was a lone cow that had wandered in through the open door!

On one occasion during my time in Ireland there was no village hall available and so we played in a barn, using the cattle stalls as dressing rooms. The mixed aroma of make-up and beasts was out of this world! It was late at night when I managed to find digs but the first words the landlady said were, 'You don't want supper, do you?' I was longing for a meal but was only too grateful to have a room. She went upstairs to get things ready and after a while called me up. On getting into bed I had a most peculiar feeling, and there was an odd smell in the air. On looking around I found a coffin with a corpse in propped up in a corner hidden behind a curtain! Needless to say, it was a very long night.

On that same tour I remember staying with a very old typical Irishman – white beard, Paddy hat and swallowtail coat – in a little whitewash cottage with a peat fire, with ducks and hens coming freely in and out of the tiny kitchen. His pigs were his pride and joy. After being there a week, I was politely asked to leave because my bed was needed for the prize pig to farrow on!

My time in rep at Leicester wasn't without its incidents either.

As usual we did two performances a night, and two plays a week. In one of those I was to play Lady Godiva and we had rehearsed a very lovely horse for the play. I will never forget one particular night when he absolutely refused to budge at the end of the scene although I furiously dug my knees into his sides to try to make him go. Eventually they had to bring down the curtain with both of us still sitting there! I was sweating so badly when I climbed off the horse that I couldn't remove the body-stocking I had been wearing (those were the days of modesty on stage!) and had to return to my digs before I could peel it off.

Another time I was playing a native girl in *White Cargo*, opposite an actor who at that time was the matinee idol. I was stretched on a couch playing the temptress and, as I pulled his head towards me, off came his toupee! I don't think anyone knew that he wore one. The scene ended with his desperate but muffled calls of, 'Curtain! Curtain! Close the curtain!'.

Again in rep, I was playing the part of a maid and Master Jack – who was my hero – was coming home from the navy. I loved him and couldn't wait to see him. The villainess says, 'Now go away! You can't be here when Master Jack comes. You're not going to see him.' As an aside to the audience I was supposed to say, 'I will see Master Jack, even if I have to peep through the key hole.' What I said by mistake was, 'I will see Master Jack even if I have to pee through the keep hole.'!

On another occasion I was playing the part of Lady Isabelle in *East Lynne*. She leaves her husband and children to go off with the villain. Her friend – Lord Mount Severn – comes to visit her and she asks him, 'Tell me, Lord Mount Severn, what of my husband? What of my children?' He is supposed to reply, 'They are all right except for the youngest, he was always a weakling. I'm sorry to tell you, but he is dying of consumption.' What he said was, 'I'm sorry to tell you, but he is dying of constipation.'!

4
PANTOS, PIERROTS AND CONCERT PARTIES

With the growth in popularity of talking films there was a corresponding slump in the theatre and for me, as for many others, things were not going very well. So, I thought about Fit Ups once again.

Desert Song was the rage, and everyone was humming the music. Things were not going very well, so on went the thinking cap. I put together a potted version, training local girls as chorus and giving any with a show of talent a small part. It was very ambitious for a local community (I believe we were at Winterton near Scunthorpe) but, although it was hard work, it paid off. As is usual with amateurs, relations and friends crowded in to see their own on stage. This gave us all quite a lift, and in the future we always tried to put on whatever was popular at the time.

By the time Christmas 1931 arrived I was gaining my first experience of professional pantomime playing principal boy in *Babes in the Wood* at the Pavilion, Worksop. Pantomime meant no Christmas fun because rehearsals went on up to Christmas Eve and the show opened on Boxing Day night. But oh, how I loved playing the children's hero! Entertaining children is always most rewarding. The following year I played principal boy again, this time just down the road from Worksop at the Grand Theatre, Mansfield. During the theatre slump, many pros had turned to weekend entertainment in workingmen's clubs. I also worked a couple of clubs in Mansfield but, although it was a help financially and paid my fare to pantomime rehearsals, clubs were not my style at all.

When summer came, I decided to try a summer season with Ran Churchill's concert party at Llandudno. I played Topsy in *Uncle Tom's Cabin*. Black minstrel shows were one of the oldest forms of open air concert party entertainment in this country. Happy Valley, Llandudno, was noted for this type of show. The parties worked on the sands, moving a portable platform and piano from site to site along the beach. It was very hard, working from eleven in the morning to nine at night. When the popularity of the minstrel shows faded, the Pierrots took over. They were concert parties which were also staged at seaside resorts. My

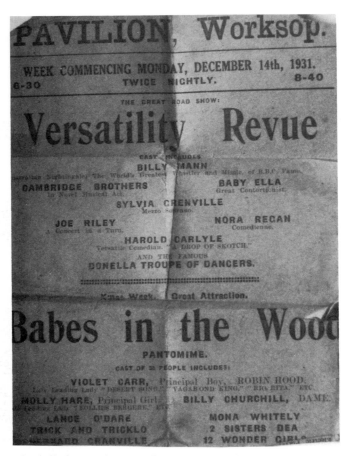

Playbill for *Babes in the Wood* – Pavilion, Worksop,
December 1931.

singing ability coupled with drama experience (for sketches) was most useful for this type of entertainment. A concert party consisted of eight *artistes* – typically a *soubrette*/dancer, a baritone, a soprano, a pianist, a duet-speciality act, and a duet-musical act. We wore Pierrot uniforms which we made ourselves: black-and-white satin with pompoms and a ruffle, and the gentlemen in long pantaloons and a little Pierrot jacket. Each manager had his own idea of what he wanted on the shows, but it was more or less the same sort of thing. With musical numbers for singles and duets, sketches and a good comedian, it was possible to put on a nice

Pierrots – Violet is front row, right.

Pierrots – Violet is 2nd from the left.

little show. Pierrots were popular because visitors could get close to the *artistes* and could take pictures. Also at the start of the season the concert party would have pictures taken, autograph them, and sell them to the patrons.

Being in the Pierrots was not a full-time living but was just for the summer season. At other times we used to do the London parks on the bandstands. That work had a longer season and, although that wasn't as enjoyable, the money was sure because you got a salary from the council. In the Beach Pierrots you sometimes got a salary, but more often you were paid a share of the receipts. One member of the party, known as the Bottler, would go around the audience collecting money in a bottle. When he counted out the takings after the show, everyone would look anxiously for 'snow' – meaning silver.

If things got a little difficult financially, there was the habitual stunt of song publishers in the summer: they put up a stage with piano at seaside resorts, and engaged a couple of singers to sing their songs. The singers would then sell copies of the songs at sixpence (2½p) each and would be paid a commission on the sales. Not surprisingly, that was sometimes not very much. I sang on many occasions for names such as Lawrence Wright, Feldman and Campbell-Connolly.

In 1934 I joined the Yorkshire Dons – a concert party managed, as I discovered, by none other than Will Godfrey – and the season opened at Sutton-on-Sea. But more about that a little later.

I remember The Dons playing at Walney Island, Barrow-in-Furness, in, I believe, 1935. We opened on Whit Monday and had only played for about a week before a gale carried the marquee off into the Irish Sea! There was no hall to transfer to and the weather was too bad for open-air performances. As a result we were stranded and decided to move on to the Lake District, to hire a hall wherever possible, and share the takings. A kindly driver interested in show biz took all of us and our props, without payment, in his coal lorry! This was indeed a blessing, even if a mixed one, and off we went not knowing where we would find a hall. We only knew we had to keep going.

We did eventually find somewhere and wrote out our own posters to advertise the show. We had only just got going when the weather changed again. This time it was too hot for indoor entertainment and as a result business was bad. We barely made enough for digs. I always remember a grocer who generously helped by selling us cheese and bread at the back door of his shop because everything was always closed by the time the show ended.

The Yorkshire Dons – Floral Hall, Hornsea 1936. Violet is 3rd from the left, and Will is 5th.

It became impossible to carry on so we had to split up. The pianist, comedian and myself were fortunate in persuading the proprietor of the Queen's Hotel, Appleby, to engage us at a very small fee to provide after-dinner entertainment to visitors staying overnight on Lakes tours. This was very pleasant but not profitable. Seeing the end in view, I wrote to a club in Mansfield where I had been very successful before, explained the situation, and asked for a date to work there again. They advanced my fare and this got me back to the Midlands.

One club date followed another and, though money was sure, it was very different from theatre work. It meant walking around clubs to audition, and a lot of your money was spent just travelling to the different towns. In addition it was not easy to perform in clubs because, as the evening wore on, the audience consumed more and more alcohol and became increasingly noisy. There were no microphones then, and to carry on singing over the noise and the smoke needed courage.

I once did some part-time singing in London nightclub cabaret. This meant working several clubs a night, doing two spots in each club, going

With The Yorkshire Dons –
Sutton-on-Sea.

Violet – Grand Theatre,
Doncaster, early 1930s.

'Throw away' photo for
fans, c.1935.

by taxi from one to another. In one club I worked for one of the more notorious proprietresses whose patrons were the cream of society. She hired *artistes* as a cover for various forms of illegal gambling including the then new 'housey-housey'. I was fated to be there one night during a police raid and had to escape by climbing through my dressing-room window. That put me off London nightclubs. I also did some work at a similar nightclub in Grimsby, which also engaged a pianist and *artiste* – again as a cover for gambling. It was easy money standing by ready to work if necessary.

For me, nothing could replace theatre. Even in these days of radio and television – and I have worked in both – there is nothing that can take the place of a theatre audience. It is sad to think that many young *artistes* of today have never experienced the live theatre nor learned the art of working without a mike; learning to deliver lines, word perfect, across an audience and up into the gallery.

Violet – London, 1937.   Nottingham, late 1930s.

In many ways London was the place to be whilst out of work because that was where the agents were. There used to be a pub in London where out-of-work pros would congregate hoping for an agent to pop in with the offer of work. It was called 'ghost walking', a very, very old expression in the business. One old trouper, so the story goes, got an engagement in Edinburgh and they all wished him goodbye and said, 'We hope the ghost walks, George', meaning they hoped that he would be paid. A couple of weeks had gone by when in walked George. 'Well', asked his pals, 'did the ghost walk?' 'Yes,' he said, 'all the bloody way back from Edinburgh!' George had been unlucky.

Even when you were fortunate enough to find stage work offering proper wages it didn't always work out because of bogus managers in the business. I remember one such experience in Portsmouth. I had been playing in rep at the King's Theatre, Southsea, the show was *Easy Virtue* – Fay Compton was in the lead role. I then moved to Portsmouth for a variety date. Variety work was a more casual type of engagement – one week here, one week there – and that was the sort of situation in which you might come across bogus managers. Come Saturday night, you might find that they had gone missing having taken all the proceeds with them, leaving the full cast stranded! This seemed to happen quite often in variety and touring theatres. There was no Equity then to protect the *artistes*, and no Social Security to turn to for support. Though I had other work to go to in Manchester, I was left with no money to get there so I did what many old pros have done and set off to walk to the next job. It was February and I wore as many clothes as possible to keep out the cold. I sent my hamper of props on the goods railway – to pay on delivery.

I was still somewhere in Hampshire, resting on a little hump bridge, when a long-distance lorry came along and stopped. The driver wondered why I looked so tired and asked me where I was bound for. Luckily he was also going to Manchester so he offered me a lift, sharing his sandwiches with me – a genuinely kind soul. As darkness came, so did a real pea-souper fog and I had to get out and guide the lorry to keep it out of the ditch. When at last I got back in, I slept all the way until I was told we were there. It was early morning, six a.m., and I was still very tired, cold and distressed. My audition was not until ten. In the distance I saw a church lit up and going over I found Mass being said (it was the custom for Lancashire mill workers to go to early Mass) so I quietly sat at the back of the church enjoying the comforting warmth. After Mass the priest came over to see me – I think at first he thought I was one of the ladies of the night who used to come into the church sometimes at that hour. When I told him of my plight, he gave me money to go and have breakfast so that I'd be in a better state for my appointment. I never knew his name but later sent a donation to the church as a thank you.

Playing in variety and revue meant touring week by week to different theatres. After a Saturday show you'd sometimes have to travel all night to be at the next town by Sunday morning. In revue the same *artistes*

Violet, c.1935.

played in various comedy sketches, whereas in variety the entertainers did different acts. It was very interesting meeting and working with so many people. I always found the foreign *artistes* to be most courteous because there were no professional jealousies – each had his or her own act.

During a long run, audiences would have their favourites, and gifts were handed over the footlights on Saturday evenings. More often than not I was given chocolates and flowers. (The old troupers' saying was, 'No flowers by request, but a Guinness would be useful!') It brought to mind the saying, 'Good girls get chocolates, bad girls get furs.' I hasten to add that it was by playing number-one theatres such as the Moss Empires and the Black circuit that I eventually got *my* fur coat!

Looking back I feel honoured to have worked with such troupers as Bransby Williams, Nellie Wallace, Charles Coburn ('The Man Who Broke the Bank at Monte Carlo'), Will Hay, and, of course, the Crazy Gang. As I said earlier, my uncle was the late Teddy Knox of Nervo and Knox of Crazy Gang fame. I am proud of his great successes and many

Bransby Williams, 1940.
One of the finest Dickensian actors, also famous
for his monologues and Churchill impersonations.

Royal Command Performances. The Crazy Gang were favourites with royalty of three generations. Teddy was another product of Portable training. It was my father who gave Bud Flanagan his famous fur coat with the idea that it would be an entertaining 'match' for his straw benger! As a child I also worked with my uncle Sax Rohmer when he was on the stage. Later he took up writing and was the creator of the sinister character, Dr Fu Manchu.

I also remember meeting Sir, then Mr, Winston Churchill. It was 1938 and I was playing at the Knightstone Pavilion in Weston-super-Mare in the thriller *Fanny by Gaslight*. Sarah Churchill was the lead and I played second to her – we were the only two ladies in the cast. Winston and Mrs Churchill were in Yeovil for a weekend house party and we met them when they came over to see their daughter's play.

Troubadour Follies playbills – Grove Park
Pavilion, Weston-super-Mare, April 1940.

In 1938 Will persuaded me to rejoin his company with a new concert
party Troubadour Follies. Until the Follies came to Weston, no ladies had
ever been allowed to entertain at the Sands Pavilion – there had only ever
been all-male shows. I was the first lady to entertain on stage there.

We did three shows a day with Troubadour Follies, and with Will's
many stunts business was good – so good, in fact, that the initial one
summer season became four, but more about the Follies in the next
chapter.

I don't know how much longer we would have continued at Weston if
it hadn't been for the War. We had been playing at the Grove Park
Pavilion because it was an indoor stage. Our other venues – the Sands
and the Winter Garden – could not be lit at night because of the black-
out. One night Grove Park itself was bombed and so the Follies run
ended.

5

WILL GODFREY

The reader has already been introduced to Will Godfrey. He was a popular entertainer in his own right and a great showman. He was my stage partner for so many years and, more importantly, my life partner, my husband. This account would be incomplete if I were not to include something of his story too.

Will was born in Stoke-on-Trent in 1892, and was first bitten by the theatre bug when he was at college training to teach mathematics. He got himself involved producing and directing college revues, even writing his own topical comedy sketches which, incidentally, he always insisted be 'clean and clever'.

His family was related to the pottery Wedgwoods and, building on his initial successes at college, Will suggested putting on a show in the form of a touring concert party and calling it *The Wedgwood Classics*, as an advertisement and promotion for the pottery. The scenery and costumes were to be in the blue-and-white Wedgwood design, and were the basis for the cameo scenes he developed. The show toured the Midlands and was a great success.

This was the point at which he gave up the idea of teaching and moved into the theatre full time. It is also the point at which we can see something of the showmanship which was to become one of his greatest assets.

In the years leading up to the First World War, he and his brother Joe did a double patter act, 'The Brothers Godfrey', on the music hall circuit where he worked with most of the music hall stars of the day. However, when War was declared, Will found himself fighting in the Somme and was in fact awarded the Croix de Guerre, although I don't remember what it was for. Blinded by mustard gas, Will was brought back to England where he was hospitalised at St Dunstan's. Thankfully his eyes healed, but every year thereafter he had to have treatment on them.

In gratitude for the care he had received at St Dunstan's, Will wrote verses on postcards which he sold in the theatres where he performed, sending the proceeds back to the hospital. At first Will was back on stage

Will Godfrey, c.1942.

with his brother, but at about this time Joe emigrated to Canada and Will went over to Ireland for a while to manage a cinema in Kilkeel. I can only assume that he must have answered an advertisement at a time when regular stage work had become scarce. When he returned he began to do drama and rep, and to run concert parties in the summer. It was when he was in rep in Newcastle that he and I first met.

In the mid-1920s Will took a drill hall at Quebec (County Durham) and brought variety acts there from Newcastle – I helped out as cashier – until the hall had to be closed when the owner's lease ran out. So Will left the area – it was the time of the national strikes – moving down to Doncaster, looking for work entertaining in workingmen's clubs, but at the same time continuing with his summer concert parties.

Between the wars Will produced the military theme revue, *Eyes Front*

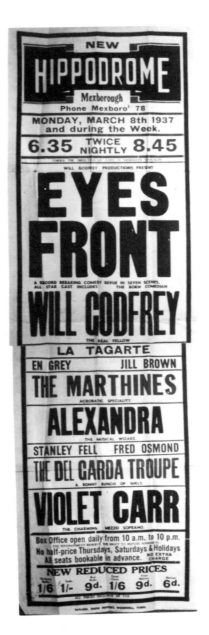

Playbill for
Will's military
revue *Eyes Front*
March 1937.

Troubadour Follies playbill – Winter Garden Pavilion, Weston-super-Mare, July 1938.

– playing the comedy character Nifty – which had a very long run including return dates, and toured most of the Yorkshire theatres for about three years. By 1934 he had put together The Yorkshire Dons concert party which was named after the River Don and was sponsored by the Yorkshire Relish company. Will had negotiated the sponsorship with the company who then provided throwaways (free gifts) in the form of cards in the shape and design of sauce bottles but containing sewing kits inside. 1934 was the year I joined The Dons and, as I said earlier, we opened at Sutton-on-Sea.

Will's idea of finding a sponsor for the company was typical of his showmanship. The managing director of the American adding-machine company, Burroughs, had taken a summer house by the sea, as wealthy people did, at Sutton. Will went along to the house to invite them to come and see the show and, of course, gave them complementary tickets. As a result, the managing director organised a weekend house party to which The Dons company was invited to provide the entertainment and, of course, we were paid. This was quite a boost for the company and for our sponsors.

The Yorkshire Dons and, later, other of Will's companies – the Weston Follies and the Troubadour Follies – toured the coastal resorts of Yorkshire, East Anglia, the south and south-west, and Wales. It was with Troubadour Follies at Weston-super-Mare that I once again joined up with Will's company.

When Troubadour Follies[1] opened at Weston-super-Mare, it was, as the *Weston Gazette*[2] pointed out, Will's twenty-first year running concert parties. It opened early in the season at the Grove Park Pavilion, and then transferred for the main part of the season to the Sands Pavilion on the beach. The Follies, which ran for four seasons, was described by the same paper as 'the brightest and most versatile concert party yet seen at the Sands Pavilion'.

It played to record audiences and took record receipts but, as one newspaper reported: 'So far this year about 30,000 people have seen the show at the Sands Pavilion – officially, that is by paying for their seats. In

[1] Programmes and posters sometimes spelled Troubadour '-our' and sometimes '-or'.
[2] Over the years the exact details of the dates of newspaper articles quoted have been lost. They are in the period 1938 to 1940.

Troubadour Follies at Beach Pavilion

Will Godfrey gives a word of encouragement to his troupe.

AFTER three disappointing weeks the talented company of Troubadour Follies at the Beach Pavilion, Hastings, had a grand night on Wednesday, when a large audience sat in the warm, calm air and enjoyed the fine entertainment and a talent contest for which excellent prizes had been given by local tradesmen.

The talent was of high standard, and the competitors, who included residents and visitors, were warmly appreciated. Prize-winners were:—

Children: 1, Terence Somerville (Hastings); 2, Lilian Pick (Chesterfield); 3, Valerie and Carol Morley. Women: 1, Mrs Webb (Reigate). Men: 1, John Murphy (Hastings); 2, Johnny Champkins (Battle).

Newspaper clipping – Troubadour Follies, Beach Pavilion, Hastings.

addition there is the "Scotsmen's Gallery" ...'. This latter comment referred to the fact that because the Pavilion was on the sands, and was open-air, frequently more people sat on the beach watching than paid to go in. The *Gazette* said that at one morning show, with about five-hundred onlookers at the sides and rear, the net proceeds were only 4s.3d.

The shows included comedians and comedy sketches, song and dance routines, musicians etc., as well as competitions for the kids at the afternoon performances. Will would then also invite star guests each week – Charles Coburn, Nellie Wallace, Sir Harry Lauder, Vivian Foster – the 'Vicar of Mirth', Ella Retford and Florrie Ford, to name but a few. The show's own programme described the Follies as 'A programme of Merriment & Jollity' for which people paid 3d, 6d, 9d and 1/- admission.

41

Autographs: Teddy Knox, Jimmy Nervo, Will Hay, Nellie Wallace, Ella Retford, Bransby Williams; Vivian Foster, and Charles Coburn.

42

In Will's press book there is a rather interesting letter:

Dear Mr Godfrey,

I am a visitor to Weston, and was at your show on Wednesday evening, your 'benefit' night. I thought it first-rate, and also that I, and the other three with me, paid very inadequately for an evening's real enjoyment.

Will you please accept the enclosed and add it to your Wednesday receipts? You all deserve an immeasurably better season than you are getting, and I hope September will give it to you. I am leaving Weston soon, but shall take away happy memories of Fred, Ron, Ken, Miss Carr, Uncle Harry, your Wizard Musician, your very able pianist, the smile of the girl who gave me a chair and a programme, and not least your own courtesy at the box.

Many thanks to the Troubadour Follies for adding zest to a holiday.
From An Anonymous Well-Wisher

He/she adds:

I think you would get a larger 'house' if you closed in the back, and so piqued the public's curiosity more.

Daily Herald Talent Competition, Weston-super-Mare, c.1938.

The visitors were marvellous, a joy to entertain, and as usual Will came up with several publicity ideas. For example, we ran talent competitions in conjunction with the *Daily Herald* – a national newspaper of the day. The paper provided beautiful gifts as prizes and we displayed their advertising matter. Another of Will's stunts, in conjunction with the

Great Western Railway, was to run children's expresses from Paddington to Weston (the return fare was all of 3s 10½d, adults 7s 9d) with a magician, ventriloquist and comedian on board to entertain the kids on the journey. On another occasion a similar train was organised from Birmingham. All this was good publicity for Weston as a resort and, being good for business, made him very popular with the council. His show broke all records for takings at the Pavilion.

This reminds me of a rather amusing incident – at least we found it amusing afterwards. Normally the takings went to the Council's safe: either Will took them or someone collected them. On one particular night the money was all ready but the person who was supposed to collect it never arrived. Will 'got his back up' and stormed down to the Winter Gardens where there was a civic function in progress. He walked out into the middle of the floor, put the money bag down right in the middle, told the Entertainments Manager what he could do with it and walked out to absolute silence! Will knew he could get away with something like that because he was making so much money for the town.

Will followed the Follies with other comedy revues and comedy pantomime. He also took it, *Eyes Front*, and his pantomimes on the road, including the North-East where he played at Seaburn, and at the Theatre Royal, Crook.

The *Weston Gazette*, *Bristol Evening Post* and *Bristol Evening World* all reported on a certain strange phenomenon, Will's legendary 'magic' sandals:

An hour or so after he (first) put them on, there was a terrific thunderstorm and a deluge. The next time he wore them, the sun was shining. Half an hour later it was raining like . . . well, it was raining like anything. On the next occasion blue skies turned to grey . . . and down came the rain. This year in the midst of the heat wave Will suddenly remembered his sandals . . . That afternoon, it rained. (*Weston Gazette*)

Whenever he puts them on it rains, and he gets a full house. He was directly responsible for the Bank Holiday storm last August. But it didn't do him much good. The audience stampeded into the pavilion and bent all the furniture. (*Bristol Evening Post*)

Apparently he once miscalculated a predicted high tide:

Mr Will ('Canute') Godfrey who can invoke the god of water simply by wearing

44

TOWN HALL, LYNTON.

Civic Night

to the " TROUBADOUR FOLLIES,"
Tuesday, July 5th, 1938.

Mr. Will Godfrey requests the pleasure of the compa

Doors open at 8 p.m.　　Commence at 8.30 p

R.S.V.P. to Miss Violet Carr, Manageress, Town Ha

Violet Carr,
MEZZO-SOPRANO.

MANAGERESS—THE " TROUBADOUR FOLLIES."
ESPLANADE PAVILION.
LYNTON and LYNMOUTH.

BOROUGH OF WESTON-SUPER-MARE.
Commercial Manager　　　　I. DAVIES.

SANDS PAVILION

★

Will Godfrey

PRESENTS

County Borough ⚜ of Sunderland.

SEASIDE DEVELOPMENT & ENTERTAINMENTS DEPT.　Telephone 56124.

J. V. CAMBURN.

Hornsea Floral Hall

ENTERTAINMENTS

Proprietors Hornsea Urban District Council

Manager for the Council J. H. W. SELLERS

Programme TWOPENCE

"THE TROUBADOR FOLLIES"

ON THE CLIFF PARK.

THE LAWN PAVILION

DAWLISH

Lessee : Will Godfrey　　　Manager : Eric Victor

NIGHTLY - 8.15 p.m.
Matinee Every Saturday 3
Wet or Inclement Weather Matinee
Daily at 3

his magic sandals, got more than he bargained for on Monday evening. (*Bristol Evening World*)

The audience had to retreat to the promenade, and the show was quite literally a wash-out!

All in all, Will's entertainment activities at Weston – in particular with the Troubadour Follies – were extremely successful both for his group of entertainers and for the town itself. As the *Weston Gazette* reported:

Mr. Will Godfrey spared no pains in popularising the sands shows last year, and now he presents a really first-class party. Admittedly, 1939 has seen tremendous strides taken in the general improvement of entertainment in Weston-super-Mare; but Mr. Godfrey appears to be one of the few individuals who has realised that without a good sands concert party, a seaside is lacking one of its greatest attractions.

High tides have been a feature of the week, and holidaymakers have enjoyed them. This picture was taken by a "Gazette" photographer at 9.15 on a very dull evening. In the foreground a little visitor has his last dig of the day, and in the background is the "islandised" Sands Pavilion, concerning which see story on page three.

Weston Gazette report of the effects of the high tide on the Sands Pavilion, Weston-super-Mare.

6

THE WAR YEARS AND LATER

With the start of the Second World War the Entertainments National Service Association (ENSA) came into being under the control of Basil Dean. Will and I were both called up and so, being firm friends by now, formed a double-patter act. He was an excellent comedian, and I was his 'feed'. We also did single acts – he as a comedy single, and me as a vocalist. In addition to lunch-time concerts with famous musicians in London and other big cities, there were also 'Music While You Work' lunch-time concerts in factories, which were broadcast on the radio. Working with ENSA meant lots of travelling without knowing where you were going (destinations were kept secret). Nor was it necessarily very comfortable work doing shows in full evening dress – in cold aeroplane hangars, for example. We shivered, but we were well repaid by the audience's appreciation. The Second World War was to make stars of many amateurs in regimental shows when it eventually ended.

There was a very bizarre incident in the early years of the War. Will had been sent by the government – we were already involved with them through ENSA – to manage a reception centre in Scunthorpe for soldiers returning to this country from the Front. It was a clearing house for the wounded and shell-shocked where they attempted to confirm identities, regiments, homes, etc. The building itself was a sort of village hall surrounded by quite extensive grounds. Will was staying in a hotel in Scunthorpe and, when he arrived this particular morning to open up the hall, he discovered a Messerschmitt 'parked' outside! Presumably it had landed during the night and had taxied for a while before tipping up nose-first in the grass. The pilot had disappeared and the plane was abandoned. Will, of course, immediately called the police and the authorities arrived and took it away on a lorry. I can remember very clearly seeing the plane myself, and some early bird souvenir hunters had already taken a few bits and pieces from it before it was removed, yet there appears to be no readily available record – in local newspapers or archives – of the plane ever having landed.

Will Godfrey

and

Violet Carr

(Comedian).

(Mezzo-Soprano).

The Favourite Comedy and Vocal Duo.

Anyway, back to ENSA. In many places we worked on after the air raid sirens went, and could feel the vibration on stage as bombs fell around us. I was in the bad raids on Birmingham and Coventry, and will never forget one particular experience. My digs in Birmingham was an old Victorian house and the air raid shelter was under the wide solid staircase. We could hear bombs falling very near and when, at last, the 'all clear' was sounded, we came out of the shelter to find the rest of the house in ruins with an unexploded bomb in the middle of the lawn. There I stood in a nightdress and fur coat, everything else gone. There was no water and no gas in the town, it was one blazing inferno. Trips out entertaining the troops seemed peaceful by comparison!

Will had taken a lease on a cinema in Cheltenham Spa (The Ritz) and had written to ask me to come and work for him as assistant manageress in charge of two shops attached to the cinema. After the bombing experience I was a nervous wreck and Cheltenham Spa was supposedly a safe area, a town full of evacuees, so I was happy to accept his offer. Male employees were difficult to find and with only a skeleton staff we were kept very busy. We joined everything to do with the war effort, and the Aid To Russia Fund, and again Will's showmanship was a great help in coming up with stunts to raise money.

The night came when Hitler's bombs again paid us a visit. It was a particularly bad raid, with much damage in town. Cheltenham would normally have been safe but close by was the firm, Smiths Clocks, which had been converted to a munitions factory. A German plane under heavy anti-aircraft fire unloaded its bombs over Cheltenham itself. I was on fire watch duty in the cinema when a huge bomb fell through the roof but didn't explode. It did, however, bring down a roof beam which fell across my leg – which felt as though it had been chopped off. I was aware that the bomb lay along the left side of my body but I was completely covered in rubble. I called out for help and eventually a warden found me. Through all the debris, I told him that I thought I had lost my leg, and in an attempt to be as light as possible under the circumstances he said, 'Never mind love, at least your watch is still ticking.' I told him that I wasn't wearing a watch – it was the bomb next to me that was ticking! Working very carefully, they removed the beam, and found that the leg was not severed but badly broken. Needless to say I was also very badly shocked.

After nine months of not being able to walk. I found I also had difficulty in breathing, and this was unusual for me given my singing ability. A specialist diagnosed a type of asthma caused by inhaling the dust from the fall of the bomb and whatever it was that I had heard escaping from the bomb as I lay next to it. He strongly advised me to leave Cheltenham and return to the more bracing air of County Durham where I had been born. This Will and I did, in 1942. So there I was after all my travelling, back in Ushaw Moor. Will and I married that year in the same Catholic church I had attended as a child – St Joseph's, Ushaw Moor.

I had been born into a very Protestant family, descendants of John Knox and, although in more recent years some of my relatives referred to me as 'the papist', I have never regretted becoming a Roman Catholic. I was brought up by Catholic foster parents, had been to Catholic schools, and went regularly to Mass. I always wondered why the other children

Violet's unexploded bomb! She was still in hospital when the photograph was taken. Will is 2nd from the left.

could go to Communion but I couldn't. I got it into my head that I must be so naughty that I wasn't allowed to go! My foster parents noticed that I was fretting over this so they approached the parish priest to see what could be done. He refused to baptise me without the consent of my actual parents who, of course, were not around. Finally the bishop gave special permission.

My faith has always been a wonderful support – after all I was in a profession with more temptations for a girl than many other walks of life. I always tried to attend Mass although when we were touring it was sometimes very difficult or even impossible. In the theatre there was always a priest-chaplain in the wings during shows to be available to anyone who might want to talk to him. Inevitably he would get quite a ribbing about being there with all the female dancers – dressed as you might expect – passing by!

Will was also a convert. During the period of time that he was operating the cinema in Kilkeel in Ireland, he had got to know the local priest very well and had spent a lot of time talking with him. He always said that it was the priest's example that encouraged him to become a Catholic.

In the North-East there was a family by the name of Black who owned theatres and cinemas – the Black circuit. George Black knew Will very well and offered him the management of two theatres in Sunderland: the Theatre Royal and the Rink. This he accepted but he had to sleep in the office at the Royal in order to be on the spot in the event of air raids. I was at Ushaw Moor living at the local pub because I was still in calliper irons as my leg had not fully recovered. We saw very little of each other and were grateful for the telephone.

Later that year, one of the two cinemas in Ushaw Moor (Club Hall Cinema in Station Road, now a dance/bingo hall) became available on lease. You didn't actually buy a cinema: the existing ones were owned by big business and they wanted people to lease and manage them on their behalf. Some of the older residents still remembered the Portable Theatre and that my mother had had this cinema for rep when I was a child actress. The miners at once took us to heart. The lessee had only kept it going as a sideline and it was a wreck, with appalling projection machines that broke down many times during shows. Will took it over and, with decent seating and decorating and plans for new machines, we were full of hopes that we would at last have a settled home and business. However, there were to be problems.

During wartime one had to have a special permit to obtain machinery of any kind and our request for new projectors was refused because it was only machinery for entertainment purposes. Not to be deterred, Will got the miners' officials together and organized a petition pleading that miners were of great importance to the war effort and as such needed relaxation for themselves and their families. They pointed out that the nearest town, Durham, was three miles away and that, with transport being so scarce, they needed entertainment closer to home. Whilst we fought for machines, posters went out to reassure the public that we would open soon. When permission was finally obtained, and an opening date was certain, Will (being the good showman he was) put on the posters that the cinema would 'definately' open by such-and-such a date, but by deliberately misspelling the word 'definitely' he ensured that people would look twice at the posters and so remember the date!

We opened to a packed house with Western Electric machines showing films in colour, a first for the village. Our old friend Tommy Trinder, who was in his prime at that time as a star comedian, sent us a telegram wishing us luck. It included Tommy's catch phrase 'Get up them stairs' and so that saying was always connected with Will in all our years there.

Once we discovered the people's taste in films, business was good –

seven nights a week with a matinee Wednesday mornings for night shift workers. Wednesday evening was Variety Night, with a pianist and local talent. Will and I supplied the comedy, and it was always a full house that night because, then as now, miners liked a good turn, and it made a welcome change from films.

The next problem we experienced was over the British Quota. British films were not at all popular with the miners and we always lost money on them but, by law, a certain quota of British films had to be shown. We had to keep a Quota Book which was sent by our accountant to the appropriate government office. When we showed American films, on the other hand, there were queues down the street and it was as a result of this that someone, jealous of our patronage, wrote to that office and falsely accused us of not keeping to the quota. As a result, we received notification that we were to be closed down. I was incensed. On the spur of the moment and ignoring Will's advice that I would never get to see him, I went down to London and, without an appointment, saw Sir Arthur Rank in person. My intention was to explain the situation to him and the fact that our quota books were in perfect order. In the event he immediately got on to the government people concerned and took care of the problem.

At the end of the War, we leased a second cinema at Penshaw and called it The Victory as we opened the night that victory was declared. Although I had a car in order to collect films from Newcastle twice a week, petrol was rationed and in very short supply. This became quite a worry and neither Will nor I was in the best of health. The climax to events came when we were involved in an accident on the Tyne Bridge when a trailer being towed by another vehicle hit us and almost knocked us over the rail of the bridge. It was a blow to our already failing health and we had to let the Penshaw cinema go. After a long spell in hospital, I discovered that I would have to have a kidney removed. It was a fight to live and Will was very distressed by it all. My illness lasted a long while during which time his own health deteriorated. There was no option but to retire, and sadly we gave up the Ushaw Moor cinema too.

During all our years in the North-East, we never refused charity work – we even entertained prisoners in Durham Prison. We started a Children's Trip Fund for the village, giving shows to raise money for a free day at the seaside, and to this day it is still in operation. It was while doing a concert for charity that Will collapsed. He was rushed to hospital where

Weston Productions

RESIDENT CONCERT
SEASONS INCLUDE:
WESTON-SUPER-MARE (3)
FOLKESTONE
SEABURN (SUNDERLAND)
WITHERNSEA (2)

R.E.C.

ALL COMMUNICATIONS TO
WILL GODFREY
LADYSMITH
USHAW MOOR
C° DURHAM

REVUE·CONCERT PARTY·PANTOMIME·VARIETY

EVERY PRODUCTION ARTISTICALLY PRESENTED

Violet and Will.

he was operated on for cancer. It was obviously only a matter of time. I nursed him alone, night and day, never leaving his bedside. I myself was in pain with a slipped disc but nevertheless I kept him in our own home where I'm sure he wished to be. On the morning of 26 May 1958, Will passed away leaving me distraught and very, very lonely.

I was alone, with very little money: we had lived on savings and had paid large sums for medical treatment and operations. Theatre work was out of the question; it would have been foolish to give up the house and travel because I could never have replaced it.

It was a very difficult period and I took any work that came my way.

53

For a while I worked for a local solicitor who also owned a farm, doing his bookwork for the farm business. However, I also had to spend long spells in traction at the hospital, and the asthma grew worse. The money was slowly giving out. I didn't know about Social Security, and it was so long since I had signed on the dole that in my depression and confusion I never gave it a thought. I pawned silver, jewellery, even my best linen. I thought (and hoped) that no one knew of my plight but someone did notice my situation and, in the nicest way, helped me. Without this help I can't think what would have become of me. That person was Father Thompson, my parish priest at St Joseph's who, in his wisdom, knew how to go about helping me without hurting my pride. How does one repay such kindness in the most desperate period of my life?

During one of my frequent periods in Maiden Law Hospital, I think it would be 1959 or '60, I met and made friends with two students from Durham University. Like me, one of them – Angie – was in the hospital in traction, and her friend Irene used to come in to visit her. After Angie was released, they both continued to come and visit me. They were not from this area and my house was home to them whenever they wished to come. Their visits gave me much happiness but eventually their time at university ended and they returned to their homes. I missed their visits so much but through the years they kept in touch. Irene now lives in Australia, but still pays me a visit whenever she in in this country.

In about 1969 I found it necessary to move from our big house (Ladysmith at the end of Ladysmith Terrace – now demolished) to a council bungalow on what were then the outskirts of the village, hoping to leave memories behind. I quickly learned that one cannot run away from oneself but, after so much travel, the peace and quiet with a lovely view of the hills was very soothing and life went on.

Early one morning I heard on the radio of my Uncle Teddy Knox's death. His second wife had died two weeks previously (his first wife was Clarice Mayne the famous music hall star) and there were no children from either marriage. I decided to enquire about his estate and engaged a solicitor. He found that there was no will and duly put in a claim on my behalf as Teddy's niece. Fortunately I still had my birth certificate, and Mam and Dad Carr had never legally adopted me. At last a silver lining seemed in view, and in due course I received my share of Teddy's estate. I immediately redeemed all the items (many of them sentimental) that I had pawned in the dark days, and good things came one after another.

At home, 1989.

By the late 1970s, my knowledge of the old Portable days came to the notice of a television producer and I appeared on the regional programme 'What Fettle?' (a Geordie series) and enjoyed it very much. In 1982 I took part in a programme on Yorkshire Telvision called, 'Where There's Life', a programme dealing not with the theatre this time but with loneliness. That was followed, in 1988, by an interview on BBC Radio Newcastle on the subject of the old Portable Theatre. After that, offers came in from various organizations to give talks on the theatre and that, too, was enjoyable.

Next I was invited to go to Sunderland's Music Hall Museum to make a tape for them about the old days, and when it unfortunately had to close I was invited to take part at The Empire on closing night. I did a talk for the Durham Amateur Dramatic Society (of which I became a member), and have had many very pleasant hours with them.

Shortly after that, someone from Cambridge University paid me a visit, taking back many notes on my theatrical experiences. It appears that the Portable Theatre is unique in theatrical history. Indeed, in January 1991, BBC Radio 4 asked permission to use an edited version of the Radio Newcastle interview as a two-part broadcast on the Portable Theatre called 'Theatre on Wheels'. I was very pleasantly surprised at the number of letters I received following that broadcast and it confirmed for me that there does seem to be an on-going interest in the history of theatre.

So, in my twilight years, it has been my good fortune to have been involved in the modern entertainment media, radio and television, and I have also contributed to a museum and to the BBC archives – which puts me in the company of many old stars, a fact of which I am very proud.

In 1982 I had to move out of my bungalow temporarily while it was being modernized. During that time I had to live in a nearby home. Apart from being a very disruptive experience, I found the size of the room they had given me very confining. As a distraction, and a way of surviving that period of time, I decided that I would sit and write an account of my life in the theatre.

I often look back at the past with wonder, and find it difficult to believe that I have done all of the things that I have. I now have just one remaining wish – that my dear parish priest will be near me at my Final Curtain.[3]

[3] Author's note: Sadly Father Thompson died on 6 September, 1989, but because in a spiritual sense it doesn't change Vi's wish, I have included this paragraph from her original (1982) account.